Crossing the River

AF673790

Om KIDZ
An imprint of Om Books International

First Published in 2023

Om Kidz | Om Books International

Corporate & Editorial Office
A-12, Sector 64, Noida 201 301
Uttar Pradesh, India
Phone: +91 120 477 4100
Email: editorial@ombooks.com
Website: www.ombooksinternational.com

Sales Office
107, Ansari Road, Darya Ganj
New Delhi 110 002, India
Phone: +91 11 4000 9000
Email: sales@ombooks.com

ISBN: 978-93-94547-20-9

Printed in India

10 9 8 7 6 5 4 3 2 1

Crossing the River

I'm all set to read

Paste your photograph here

My name is

Mr. Green the **grasshopper**, wanted to **cross** the **river**.

He wanted to see **what there** was on the **other** side of the **river**.

His best **friend** Bernie **said**,
"I'm sure you'll **find** exactly
the same things we **have here**.
It **will** be sunny **with** lots of
grass and giant **leaves** to eat!"

Mr. Green **said**, "But I often hear strange noises coming **from** the **other** side of the **river**.

I wonder **what that is.**"

Bernie had **heard** the noises too. He **said**, “Yes, I **would** love to **find** out.

But how will we **cross** the **river**? We can **only** fly **very** short distances."

“I think **that** if we could find a big **leaf** we can **push** it **into** the **water**. We can sit on it and get across the **river**,” **said** Mr. Green.

He had a lot of good ideas!
“That’s a great plan, buddy!
I will get a big **lotus leaf**
tomorrow.

We **both** can easily sit on it."

The next morning, the two **grasshoppers** met at the riverside. Bernie had **brought** a large **lotus leaf with** him. He was out of breath **pulling** it.

The two **grasshoppers pushed** it hard **into** the **water**. **Then they both hopped** onto the leaf. It began to **float** slowly.

Bernie **said**, "You **know what**? We should use long stems to **push** the **water** so **that** the **leaf** can **move** faster."

A **very** fast motor **boat** passed **them** by. The **leaf** was light and so it **turned** over.

The two **friends** fell **into** the river. They started **flapping their wings very** fast.

Then Mr. Green **spotted** two **bulls** **bathing** in the **river**.

The **grasshoppers** **flew** and sat on **their** backs.

But the **bulls were** wet **from** the bath in the **river**.

The two **grasshoppers** started **slipping** and **sliding** off. “We **have** to move **from** here,” yelled Mr. Green. Bernie **nodded** his **head**.

They flew off and sat down in a **boat** filled **with humans**.

"**They** are **carrying drums**," **said** Bernie. The **boat** reached the **other** side of the **river**.

The **humans** set up the **drums** and began **playing** as soon as the Sun set. “So, that’s the sound **coming from** across the **river**,” **said** Mr. Green excitedly.

The two **grasshoppers danced** happily all **night** to the **human** music.

Know Your Words

Sight Words

both
find
from
have
here
into
know
only
other
over
said
that
then
them
there
their
very
were
what
with
will
would

Naming Words

bulls
boat
drums
friend
grass
grasshopper
humans
head
leaf
leaves
lotus
night
river
water
wings

Doing Words

bathing
brought
carrying
coming
cross
danced
flapping
flew
float
heard
hopped
move
nodded
playing
pulling
push
pushed
sliding
slipping
spotted